THE PONY EXPRESS

by Darice Bailer

Illustrated by Tom Antonishak

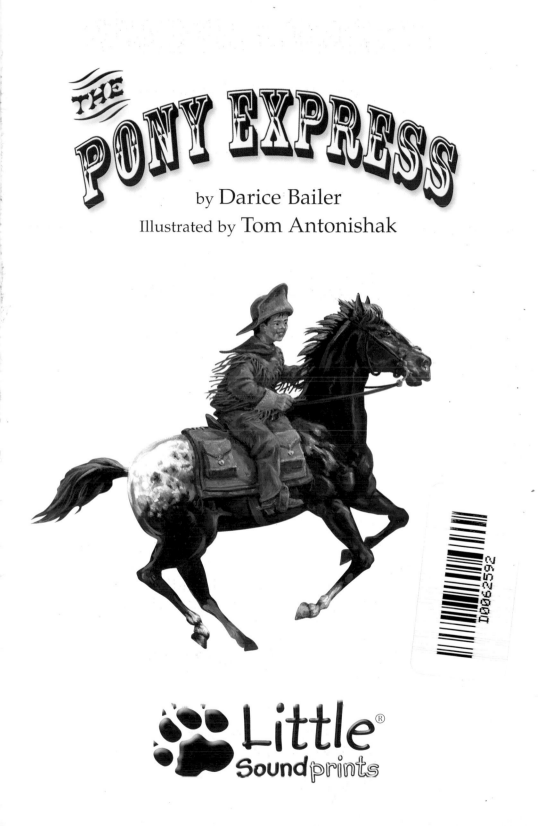

Little®
Soundprints

In memory of Charles Tyler Hill
August 3, 1990 – January 13, 1996

Like Pony Express riders, Tyler was young and brave. He contended with a malignant tumor rather than bandits or mountains. And yet, he would grin from beneath his favorite Batman hat and flash "I love you" in American Sign Language with the fingers of his right hand. He rides on in our hearts. — D.B.

To my wife, Carol, and children, CaryAnn and Tom. May you always be adventurous. — T.A.

Published by Soundprints Division of Trudy Corporation, Norwalk, Connecticut.

Book design: Marcin D. Pilchowski
Editor: Laura Gates Galvin
Editorial assistance: Chelsea Shriver

First Edition 2003
10 9 8 7 6 5 4 3 2 1
Printed in China

Acknowledgments:
Soundprints would like to thank Ellen Nanney and Robyn Bissette at the Smithsonian Institution's Office of Product Development and Licensing for their help in the creation of this book.

Library of Congress Cataloging-in-Publication Data is
on file with the publisher and the Library of Congress.

Table of Contents

A note to the reader:
Throughout this story you will see words in **bold letters**.
There is more information about these words in the
glossary. The glossary is in the back of the book.

Chapter 1
Ponies and Bandits

"It only took ten days to deliver the mail?" asks Emma.

"I could have delivered the mail faster than that!" exclaims Kevin.

"Kevin, there were no airplanes or mail trucks back then. I'd like to see you deliver mail from Missouri to California on a pony in less than ten days!" says Lucy.

Kevin, Lucy, Tomas and Emma are at the Smithsonian Institution's National Postal Museum in Washington, DC.

Emma is reading about the Pony Express. In 1860 and 1861, brave young men carried the mail, newspapers and important information by pony.

"Look at this!" shouts Emma.

A video is playing on a large screen inside the doorway of a log cabin model.

"I was on the first Pony Express run," a man is saying.

Tomas, Lucy and Kevin rush over to see the video. The man says his name is Warren Upson, but his nickname is Boston.

The man tells how he pulled his pony through floods and snow. Boston then puts his cap back on his head. "Gotta ride, partners!" he says.

As Kevin turns away from the screen, he gasps at what he sees!

Kevin is no longer in the museum. He is outside, and in the distance he sees mountains.

"It's time to saddle up and head out, Boston," Kevin hears a man say.

The man is leading a mustang pony toward Kevin. All at once, Kevin realizes the man is talking to him. The man thinks *he* is Boston Upson!

Just then, a rider gallops toward them.

"Trail is clear," says the rider to the stationmaster. "There are no robbers or horse thieves tonight. They wouldn't dare hold up the Pony Express!"

"Bob, I think those bandits learned their lesson on that last ride," the stationmaster says. "Bob was brave, wasn't he, Boston?"

Kevin nods, but he has no idea what the stationmaster is talking about! He can't wait to find out what happened to Bob.

"I didn't see those bandits until I came around a curve on the trail," Bob says. "And there they were: two bandits sitting on their ponies just waiting for me. Their guns were pointed at my chest!"

"What happened next?" Kevin gasps.

Chapter 2

The Important Message

Bob continues his story.

"Throw up your hands or you're a dead man!" they said. "Give us your pony and the mail!"

The stationmaster whistles and Bob takes a deep breath.

"I told the bandits they would have to catch me before I would give them anything! And before they could fire a shot, my pony and I were gone!"

"I shouldn't keep you any longer with my talking," says Bob. "South Carolina soldiers fired their guns at Fort Sumter. There's a war on!"

Kevin realizes Bob must mean the **Civil War**! Bob pats the ***mochila***, the bag in which the mail is carried. "There's an article from a South Carolina newspaper inside that tells what happened. Boston, you've got to make good time on this run. Since your father is the editor of the Sacramento *Union* newspaper, he'll want this news right away."

"So the war between the states has finally begun," the stationmaster says, shaking his head. "It's up to you now, Boston, to bring this sad news to California."

Kevin can't believe he is going to deliver such important news all the way to California. And, on a pony!

"Hurry, Boston," Bob says. "And don't let the snow bury you in those mountains!"

Chapter 3
Ready to Ride

Kevin swings himself up onto the pony's back. His heart pounds fast. He has never been on a horse or a pony before, but somehow he knows just what to do. He digs in his heels.

"Whoa, Boston!" the stationmaster shouts. "Not so fast. I have to record the time you leave." He scratches the time on a time log with a **quill pen**. Then he tucks the time sheet into the *mochila* and locks it.

Then the stationmaster looks at Bob and says, "Nice job. You arrived one hour early from your run. That should help Boston if he runs into trouble on the mountains."

"Do you think you can keep up a fast pace, Boston?" the stationmaster asks Kevin.

"If Bob completed his run early, I can do the same!" says Kevin.

"That's not so easy, Boston," the stationmaster says.

Kevin is confused. "Why isn't it easy?" he asks the stationmaster.

"Because you have a long ride ahead of you—almost sixty miles! Although, I am forgetting how fast you and the other riders delivered President Lincoln's inaugural speech. It took only seven days and seventeen hours!"

"And I am going to help beat that now," Kevin says, lifting his hat and galloping away.

"I can't believe I'm riding a pony!" Kevin hollers. He wishes his friends could see him now!

Chapter 4

Through Rain, Sleet and Snow

Suddenly, Kevin's eyes open wide. Right in front of him is a pack of wolves. The wolves are howling and they look hungry and mean.

Kevin's heart pounds in his chest. The wolves circle him and his pony. They snarl and bare their teeth.

"Let's get out of here!" yells Kevin. He snaps the reins and the pony gallops down the trail, just ahead of the wolves.

Soon, the wolves are far behind and Kevin lets the pony slow down.

Kevin pats the pony. "I'm glad you're fast. Those wolves sure looked hungry!"

As they ride farther up into the mountains, it begins to snow. A gusty wind blows the snow around as they ride. Icy flakes sting Kevin's face and hands. He shivers from the cold.

The pony continues along as if he has been on this trail many times before.

"It's a good thing you know the way," Kevin tells the pony. "The trail markings are hidden under all this snow."

At times, the snow is so deep that Kevin climbs off his pony and leads him through the drifts.

Kevin is cold and hungry, but he knows he can't quit.

"When you're a Pony Express rider, you have to follow the oath," Kevin says, talking out loud to his pony. "No swearing, no drinking and you must think about the mail first, your pony second and yourself third."

"I must go on. I must go on," Kevin repeats to himself. "If I don't reach the next station, how will people ever know that the Civil War has begun?"

Finally, Kevin and his pony reach the other side of the mountain. As they make their way down toward the valley, the snow turns into heavy rain. Kevin is soaked.

"Delivering the mail isn't easy," Kevin tells his pony. "No wonder the Pony Express uses the best ponies, like you!"

Kevin charges into Yank's Station. The stationmaster hands him a mug of coffee. He drinks it fast. The mug warms his cold hands. As soon as he finishes drinking, Kevin hops back on his pony and gallops away!

Chapter 5

End of the Journey

When Kevin reaches the **American River**, the water spills over the banks. Kevin needs to get across the river, but he doesn't see a bridge. He has no choice but to wade across the river with his pony.

Kevin hops off the pony and removes the *mochila*. He holds it high over his head. He must keep the mail from getting wet.

Finally, Kevin reaches the other side of the river. He and his pony are soaked, but the mail is dry!

Soon Kevin arrives at Strawberry Station. The stationmaster has a new pony ready for the next leg of the journey.

Kevin is tired and hungry, but he knows that Pony Express riders can only stop for two minutes at each station.

Kevin tells the stationmaster the news of the war.

"The President is going to need help fighting to preserve the Union," the stationmaster says. "I'd better join the Union troops."

Kevin knows that if it hadn't been for the Pony Express, it could have been weeks before this man heard about the war!

Kevin gulps down some water from a tin cup and quickly eats a piece of cornbread. Then he gallops away once more.

He hopes he can make it in record time. The sky is clearer and the ground is drier than it was in the mountains.

Eleven miles later, Kevin reaches Webster's Station. He switches ponies again and picks up new mail. Twelve miles later, Kevin does the same at Moss Station and heads toward Sportsman's Hall—his last stop.

Kevin is so tired that he almost falls off his pony. He tries to keep his eyes open. The stationmaster turns to speak to a man walking out of the station.

"Sam, it's time for you to take over. Get this mail to Sacramento!"

"Trail's clear," Kevin says to Sam, repeating what Bob said to him.

Sam lifts his hand in a salute to Kevin and the stationmaster.

"Hurry, Sam!" Kevin shouts. "You're carrying important news!"

Chapter 6
The Bravest of All

"Now you go inside and eat, Boston," the stationmaster says to Kevin. He pats Kevin on the back. "You've got two days to rest before Sam returns. Then you'll be heading back east. Who knows what news Sam will bring us."

Inside the cabin, Kevin takes some steaming oatmeal from a black pot above the fire. He is happy he can finally rest. He closes his eyes for a moment.

Suddenly, Kevin hears laughter. He opens his eyes and looks around. He is back in the museum!

"True or false?" Tomas asks, reading the display case. "Buffalo Bill was one of the most daring Pony Express riders."

"False," says Kevin.

"You're right," Tomas replies. "It says here that they aren't sure that Buffalo Bill actually rode the Pony Express. But how did you know that?"

Kevin smiles and points to the video. The man who is portraying Boston Upson is once again telling his story.

"It had to be him," Kevin says. "Boston Upson was the bravest of all!"

Glossary

American River: a river in California that runs down from the Sierra Nevada Mountains and empties into the Sacramento River in Sacramento.

Civil War: a war fought in the United States from 1861-1865. The Union, or northern states, fought the Confederacy, or southern states. The Confederacy broke off and formed its own government for economic and political reasons.

Mochila: (pronounced mo-CHEE-la) the leather saddle cover that fits over a pony's regular saddle. Pony Express riders rode on top of the *mochila*, which was used to carry mail and other documents.

Quill pen: a pen made from a feather. The quill was carved to form a point and dipped in ink for writing.

Stagecoach: a four-wheeled carriage pulled by several horses. The coach carried mail, packages and people over long distances, averaging 4-5 miles per hour.

About the Pony Express

In 1860, a half a million people lived in settlements in California, Nevada and Utah. These pioneers didn't want to wait three weeks for mail to arrive by **stagecoach**, or up to six months for the mail to arrive by ship. When a civil war threatened to divide the nation, the people demanded quicker mail and news.

On April 3, 1860, the Pony Express mail service began to provide settlers with faster service. Brave young men carried mail, news and government documents on pony. They rode 1,966 miles from St. Joseph, Missouri, to Sacramento, California, with the mail in just ten days. They earned $25 a week.

Riders and ponies formed a truly courageous team. Even though they faced great danger on their mail runs, only one rider died and only one *mochila* of mail was lost.

The transcontinental telegraph was completed on October 24, 1861. Now messages could be transmitted across the country in one day and at a cheaper price than the Pony Express.

Two days after telegraph operation began, the Pony Express mail service ended. It lasted just 18 months, but proved that communication across the western wilderness was possible in all seasons.